Marketing A Great New Product!

by Ken Ninomiya

Marketing A Great New Product. First Printing. ISBN# 978-0-9827374-2-2
Miramar, Florida 33029   U.S.A.
All rights reserved.
©Copyright 2012. ekn links. by Ken Ninomiya.

For information about this work, please contact Publisher at the email address info@eknlinks.com
Please check our website for any material updates. www.30PageUniversity.com

30 PAGE UNIVERSITY

About the Author

Ken Ninomiya (The Small Biz Pilot)

Prof. Ken Ninomiya (aka The Small Biz Pilot) specializes in developing and implementing results-oriented sales and marketing programs for global manufacturers. Prof. Ken has conducted a number of hands on global seminars for business growth and is the founder and VP of ekn links and smallbizpilot.com, an award winning strategic management and consultant firm dedicated helping to grow small business. He has held Director level positions at Dole Products, a Revlon Licensed company and has also helped to establish the U.S. office of one of the largest confectionery and food manufacturers in South America.

Prof. Ken caught the entrepreneurial spirit from the young age of twelve, tutoring for neighborhood kids to buy video games, and then opened a toy and hobby shop by the age of 18. Prof. Ken has 25+ years of sales and marketing experience in positioning global consumer products, service business and specification products for growth. Part of his international experience includes a residency in Shanghai, China where he helped companies understand the U.S. market and was given an honorary appointment as the Trade Liaison to the Zhei-Bei district of Shanghai. With the understanding of Spanish and Mandarin Chinese, Ken Ninomiya holds a degree from Dallas Baptist University and an Executive MBA from Chapman School of business, Florida International University.

As an academic, Ken has accomplished state championship titles for International Business plans and Salesmanship and has been awarded the Richard Boulware Scholarship for entrepreneurship. Prof. Ken is currently a visiting professor of business and marketing in graduate studies. In 2010, Prof. Ken developed a system to help educate children ages seven to twelve about entrepreneurship, life and family while authoring two educational work books, "Rusty's Lemonade Stand" and "Suki's Short Summer" under the "BizEBunch.com" banner. This new business series of 30 Page University workbooks is designed for all levels of adults from the pro to the beginner to help them improve their business.

Every 30 Page University book is supported online with podcast, video lessons, worksheets and additional free tools. Visit www.30PageUniversity.com for more information.

Look for additional titles about business, entreprenuership and management at most online book retailers and at www.30PageUniversity.com.

Visit www.kenninomiya.com to learn more.
Visit www.smallbizpilot.com to view projects and case studies.
Visit Facebook.com/smallbizpilot
Join my blog at www.profken.us

Dedication

This book is dedicated to all of the business minded entrepreneurs and to those who have yet to make the leap. To those who want to innovate and create a great new product. To those who have a great idea to share with the world. Realize your dream!

I would like to offer a special dedication to my wife, Beth, who is a great consumer of products but an even better supporter of my goals. This book is also dedicated to my kids Suki, Rusty, and Chiquita, who are blessed with the promise of a bright future and who are destined to improve our world.

...and now a word from our sponsor, SmallBizPilot.com

Prof. Ken started Small Biz Pilot to help focus on building opportunities for small businesses and entrepreneurs. The Small Biz Pilot team creates customized programs to assist small business partners in the development of their sales and marketing efforts and to help execute their global go-to-market strategy. We can help with E-Marketing, Product Development, Marketing Development, Sales Development, Global Growth and Business Strategy.

The Small Biz Pilot Team applies tested best practices and pure intellectual capital to provide alternatives to our partners. We create interest in your company, product or service from the ground up. We can get you to market, deliver the management support and provide the intellectual capital to grow your business.

© 2012 ekn links. Ken Ninomiya

How To Use This Book Successfully.

The 30 Page University series of books are made for levels from the beginning business executive to the most experienced. This hands-on-book provides the reader an easy-to-understand review of some of the most vital business functions required to succeed for any small business.

Read. There are 10 pages in this book with the Read Icon. This is the illustrated section of the book that helps you to recognize the business challenge. This illustrated section is based on a real-life event and will probably have some similarities to a close personal situation of your own.

Learn. This section includes 10 Learn pages of detailed information and topic lessons. This information is abridged to quickly encompass all of the lesson. This section will help you to learn some of the fundamental topics of the books subject.

Do. These 10 Do pages are your hands on lesson. Use these pages to practice what you have learned throughout the book. It may be a bit old fashioned but if you take the time to write down your thoughts about each section that is covered, it will help to formulate your plan. The first step of a plan is to have one. You will need to start by writing down some ideas.

Most business concepts are complex but this book series helps to break through the clutter and narrows it down to key components for every business manager. The goal of this series is to inform the reader, educate the reader and help them to execute the ideas on each topic to make the reader a better business manager.

The 30 Page University format is easy to follow and every topic is covered in just 30 Pages. You will learn a valuable skill at the completion of every 30 Page University book. This skill can be used in your business environment today to make you more successful.

Every 30 Page University book is supported online with podcast, video lessons, worksheets and additional free tools. Visit www.30PageUniversity.com for more information.

To successfully use this book you must:
    1: Complete each section of the book : Read, Learn and Do.
    2: Complete the worksheets contained in the "DO" section of the book.
    3: Put what you have learned into practice in your business today.

That's it! It's this simple to learn a new skill in your business. You will be eligible for a certificate upon completion of this book and implementation in your business.
Go online at www.30PageUniversity.com to learn more.

 Read. There are 10 pages in this book with the Read Icon. This is the illustrated section of the book that helps you to recognize the business challenge. This illustrated section is based on a real-life event and will probably have some similarities to a close personal situation of your own.

Notes:

Mr. Z was a lucky guy. He lost his job a year earlier but that resulted in his attempt to come up with a business of his own. On a holiday trip to a land far away, Mr. Z came across a small local village that bottled its own water from a local fresh water well.

Since all tourists at this far-away land only drank this bottled water, Mr. Z did the same. The water was incredible. It was one of the best tasting, fresh bottled waters that Mr. Z had tasted. He learned through the locals in the village that this water was special because it was bottled right from the fresh waterfall from the Mountain of Life. It had been said that this water helps with the villagers' health and that all of the villagers drink this water because they believe in the legends of the Life Water.

Mr. Z needed to bring this water into the U.S. market. He met with the local owner of the bottle factory and soon they agreed that Mr. Z would have the rights to market this water in the U.S. . The bottle factory owner told Mr. Z that he cannot support this market attempt financially, but will send him some samples to help him begin the market entry. Mr. Z now needed to figure out how he can bring this water into the U.S. marketplace.

Mr. Z was aware that many new products fail. He also knew that new products that try to enter into the U.S. marketplace fail. He realized that for his idea to succeed, he needed to come up with a strong strategy. He remembered that to create a strong strategy he would need to develop a good marketing plan but he did not think he would need one.

A marketing plan will help Mr. Z understand his target audience, the product positioning, and the proper packaging that will be needed as well as the best price that could be charged. The Life Water was a great product that no one else had. Mr. Z did not need to have a great strategy because he had a great product. Mr. Z started to think about a marketing strategy but in the end he did not create a marketing plan. He believed that he could enter the U.S. market without the use of a plan as long as he had a great product and a good price.

Mr. Z decided to invest all of his retirement savings into his new business idea and worked hard to get Life Water into the U.S. market. He opened up a business and secured some local warehouse space. Mr. Z contacted the bottle factory in the far away land and he placed his first order for 1,000 cases of Life Water. The new Life Water company was now on its way.

The order for 1,000 cases of Life Water would be in the U.S. in sixty days. Mr. Z. could not believe how easy it was to place the order and start up his great new Life Water company. He was now ready to start to sell his new product but he really did not have a plan. Mr. Z thought that it should not be hard to sell water. He realized that everyone drinks water and everyone will surely like his product.

Mr. Z started to search the internet for some information. He searched out some other waters that are currently sold in the market. He looked at all of the prices in the market and was happy to see that his water could be priced lower than all of them. He calculated that if he bought the water for only .20 cents per bottle that he could sell the water for .70 cents per bottle to everyone. This price would be great! Mr. Z will make .50 cents per bottle.

With this price set in mind, Mr. Z started to search the internet for some buyers that would buy his product. He quickly came across the web sites for several large retail stores that would make great customers for Mr. Z. He was able to locate some information about them and sent out an email to introduce himself and the new Life Water.

Within only two weeks Mr. Z was able to get an appointment with a local buyer. The local buyer was a smaller distributor but Mr. Z thought that if he could just sell a few hundred cases of his water that he would be starting his business.

Mr. Z prepared a small presentation on his computer about his new Life Water product and he showed it to the buyer during his meeting. The buyer was impressed with this new water but really was not sure it would work in the U.S. market. The buyer asked Mr. Z about his marketing plan and Mr. Z told her that it is only water so a marketing plan is not so useful. Mr. Z explained that everyone drinks water and this water is special because it is super healthy for you!

The buyer was still not sure about the New Life water but wanted to give it a try. She told Mr. Z that if she buys it for .70 cents than she must sell it for .95 cents. She also asked Mr. Z for a discount on the first order and extra time to pay for it. Mr. Z agreed and he sold his first 200 cases of Life Water.

With the immediate success of getting the first small order, Mr. Z went to the SuperMart office and had a meeting with one of the buyers there. The buyer was nice enough but asked many questions about the product, the price, the marketing and the strategy of the product. Mr. Z explained to the buyer that it's only water and all of that information is not required.

The buyer was surprised to hear that type of response and informed Mr. Z that he could not buy the product yet if Life Water does not have these important steps figured out. Mr. Z was surprised to hear that but understood that the SuperMart buyer probably did not understand how great this water was. The buyer also told Mr. Z that the price was not the best possible price and that SuperMart would have to get better pricing than most retailers. The buyer also said that maybe after Mr. Z has more information about who wants this product and who would buy it, he would consider putting Life Water in the stores. Mr. Z told the buyer that he thinks that everyone needs water and that the price is the best possible. Mr. Z thanked the buyer and walked away without an order.

I think that our price is fair. Everyone could buy this water. I hope you will buy in the future.

This Life Water looks OK but who will buy this water? Why would they buy it? The price seems high. I don't think we can buy this now. Maybe sometime in the future when you have more success.

Does he know the target market? Who will buy this?

Within three months, Mr. Z had a warehouse full of Life Water. He had visited many buyers over the past two months and had limited success. He was still sure that his product would sell, but did not know exactly how he would do it.

He thought it would be easier to sell this great new product. Mr. Z did not realize that the buyers required more information about how the product would be marketed. He remained positive but started to worry a bit because he invested all of his money into this new product idea. Mr. Z started to come up with some other ideas to help sell his water.

He would make an attempt to sell his water to local schools and local hospitals. Mr. Z figured that they must be able to buy his water. After all, why would they not want a water that was healthy for you and that comes directly from the Mountain of Life? Mr. Z contacted a friend who works at a local school and was able to get an introduction to the board. He thought that they would be able to pay even more money for the water so he raised the price to .90 cents per bottle. Mr. Z thought that with a higher price he could make back some of the money he had been losing the last three months.

Mr. Z went to meet with the school buyers and together they discussed the Life Water product. Most of the buyers were impressed but many of them did not see what made Life Water so different than the water they currently were using.

The school buyers also noted that the price of this water was much higher than the current water they were buying. The school buyers declined the water and advised Mr. Z to come back when he has a water that is different than what they have now and meets their price range.

Although discouraged from the meeting Mr. Z focused on the next meeting with the buyers from the hospital. Unfortunately, that meeting did not turn out any better and Mr. Z walked away with no business. Mr. Z did not understand why he could not get anyone to buy into his product. He knew it was great but had to convince others of it. Mr. Z needed to come up with answers fast. He was running out of time and money.

More than six months have passed, and Mr. Z still has a warehouse full of Life Water. He had been to many different buyers over the last six months with very little success. He was running out of money and he had little time to start making sales. His mind was full of "what if's" and questions that he could not find the answers to.

He never thought that it would be so hard to sell water. Mr. Z started to put the blame on himself and tried to understand what he could do differently to sell his water.
He came up with some ideas that all lead to a marketing strategy. He started to realize that he needed to develop a plan that will help him get this water out to market.
He remembered back to day one of his venture and started to realize that his first mistake was not having a marketing strategy and plan.

Later that day, Mr. Z got a call from his local distributor who did buy some Life Water a few weeks before. The news was not good. The buyer told him that the Life Water had not been selling. Mr. Z was completely crushed at this point. The only customer he sold his product to is now complaining that it is not selling. The buyer was kind enough to tell Mr. Z that they would continue to sell this product but they needed him to bring in some type of marketing plan to help them sell this Life Water. Together, they discussed some ideas and Mr. Z was writing everything down. During this call Mr. Z realized that selling the product to the distributor is only the first step to building a product. The most important step is helping the distributor sell the product that they buy.

Mr. Z collected his notes from his discussion with the buyer and started to think through some ideas to help him with his marketing efforts. He was not an expert at marketing so he consulted with a local marketing strategy company to discuss some ideas.

The first step in the strategy was to outline some goals that needed to be achieved quickly. Goal number one was to sell more product. Mr. Z was able to review some great ideas and together with the marketing team, they put a plan together.

Mr. Z realized he was wrong in his belief that anyone would automatically buy this Life Water product and he underestimated the complexity of selling a seemingly simple product. After two weeks, Mr. Z was able to put together some specific ideas for his distributor and personally delivered them. The ideas were well received and the buyer was now refocused on the Life Water products. Mr. Z left that meeting with a better understanding of how he needed to promote his products.

Mr. Z was now also refocused on his Life Water product. He went back to his office to review some additional ideas that were developed during his meeting with the marketing team. Mr. Z started to choose those ideas that he thought would make the quickest impact and he worked to make these ideas happen fast.

Mr. Z realized that he had to start from the beginning. That included developing a marketing plan for his product. Together with the marketing team, they worked on a plan that included a marketing strategy, a promotional plan and a pricing strategy.

Mr. Z was able to include some of the things he learned before he had a plan but as he organized his thoughts the plan started to come together. Focusing on the basic items needed, like a target market, a unique selling proposition and a better understanding of the competition, Life Water was ready to go back into the market. The one item that Mr. Z did not consider during his enthusiasm in getting the product to market was understanding the market through more research. It was a great relief knowing what the opportunity looked like after Mr. Z and his team completed the market research.

He worked on a specific strategy to help get the Life Water product out to the market. Mr. Z was able to create a promotional plan that he would use when he got the product to market and he knew how much money he would have to spend to get this product to market. Now with the proper research done and with a fully designed marketing plan, he was more confident in his ability to get the product to market. Mr. Z realized that a marketing plan did not guarantee his success but now he had a strategy that he could use to help him get closer to success.

 **Learn.** This section includes 10 Learn pages of detailed information and topic lessons. This information is abridged to quickly encompass all of the lesson. This section will help you to learn some of the fundamental topics of the books subject.

Notes:

The next ten pages include these quick easy to learn lessons:

Lesson #1 What is your USP (Unique Selling Proposition)? Be Different. Be Unique.

Lesson #2 Identify your S.W.O.T. (Strengths, Weaknesses, Opportunities and Threats)

Lesson #3 Who is your Competition? Where are they?

Lesson #4 Let's Look at the World.

Lesson #5 Know Who your Customers are.

Lesson #6 Your Price and Position mean something.

Lesson #7 Know your Cost.

Lesson #8 Promote. Discuss. Share.

Lesson #9 Getting Your Product to Market.

Lesson #10 You Are Your Best Promoter!

Lesson #1: What is your USP? (Unique Selling Proposition) Be Different. Be Unique.

Imagine a world of duplicates. Every car is the same, every house is the same, every man, woman and child are the same. If you can visualize this, you probably would not like it very much. Now take this same concept and apply it to a product or service. Imagine if all Mexican food taste the same in every restaurant, imagine if every airline flight you took offered the same service, imagine if every toy for our children was the same toy.
This makes for a boring world and a boring new product.

A marketer's new product must be different. Most successful marketers will find a need or a niche that is not yet filled and work to fill it. Marketers look to make something different while providing innovation to a marketplace. This point of differentiation and drive in innovation will separate your new product from the competition.

Marketers must first understand their point of differentiation while mapping this uniqueness out within the strategy of the marketing plan. Knowing how the product is different than what is already offered is vital to a product's success. Differentiation is a very important concept in marketing. This must be thought through completely. A marketer must be able to easily define the **unique selling proposition (USP)** of what makes their product different. Why would someone buy your product? Why is it different?

Basic Business Strategies

- Be Different.
- Be Low Price.
- Be High Tech.
- Be High Price.

There are four basic business strategies. Choosing one will help you gain a competitive advantage and make you unique.

Differentiation can come in many forms. If you're a service business, you can be different by your operating hours, service expectations, performance expectations, actual service deliverable, and pricing. If you have a product, you can be different in product shape, size, packaging, product expectations, performance and price. There are many ways to make your offering different but a marketer must decide on how to do this. This **unique selling proposition (or differentiation)** will help to determine your place in the market. The marketing mix and the marketing strategy will be dictated by your product differentiation. *Remember, marketers must make it different, make it unique and make it their own.*

Lesson #2 : Identify your S.W.O.T (Strengths, Weaknesses, Opportunities and Threats)

You may have heard of "S.W.O.T." before but do you understand it? Before a marketer maps out a marketing strategy, it is necessary to understand how the world will affect their business and how their business will affect the world. A good S.W.O.T. allows marketers to identify their own **STRENGTHS, WEAKNESSES, OPPORTUNITIES and THREATS (S.W.O.T).** A good S.W.O.T. will also help to identify the same for the competition. A marketer must use a S.W.O.T. analysis to understand the competition and their own opportunity. This S.W.O.T. analysis allows marketers to know what they are up against, where improvements need to be made, allow visibility into market opportunities and prepare for future events that may affect the business. A typical S.W.O.T. reviews both the external environment and the internal environment while allowing the marketer to identify market opportunities.

Internal Environment Review

Personal reflection can reveal the good, the bad and the ugly of life. A S.W.O.T is often used as an opportunity to see the market as if we are looking into a mirror, specifically when we review the strengths and the weaknesses of our situation.

As we prepare to examine our own company **STRENGTHS and WEAKNESSES** we must look inside ourselves. This internal review evaluates what we do well and what we do not do well. **Strengths** include items like personal customer attention, a unique application or use of an item that no one else has and even good pricing position can be a strength. A **weakness** will also be internal. **Weaknesses** should include items like lack of experience, limited financial resources and small market reach. Both your strengths and weaknesses are looked at as if you are looking into a mirror. Identify your internal strengths and weakness during your S.W.O.T. review.

External Environment Review

Marketers can control the internal processes, and their own strengths and weaknesses but it is hard to control those events that happen outside of the controllable environment. The **OPPORTUNITIES and THREATS** analysis reviews what occurs outside of a marketer's control, the external review. **Opportunities** can often be described as opening new locations in new markets, creating new services to serve new customers or even building on a promising brand position. **Threats** are often reviewed as changes in the marketplace, consumer needs, or changes in how things are normally done within your marketplace. Competition is always a threat so listing a competitor in this section will not help a marketer prepare for something outside the norm. A marketer should always be prepared to consider competition as a threat. The S.W.O.T. analysis helps to identify the competition.

Competitive Review

You will also need to **create a S.W.O.T. for your competitors** in the marketplace. Identify three competitors within your market that you can measure your performance against. Choose from the largest competitor, the most local and also the smallest competitor. Understanding how the competition operates will help you succeed in your business. When you have identified three competitors, you should do a S.W.O.T. analysis on each one of them.

Lesson #3 : Who is your Competition? Where are they?

A marketer must get to know who the competition is and what they do in the market. Using a S.W.O.T. analysis for each of the competitors will help to identify them. Knowing how your competition will react when you enter the marketplace is a vital component of being able to penetrate and secure your share of the market.

Suppose you are inventing or creating a new product. Then you would naturally assume that there is no competition. This may be a safe assumption but how long will it be before you have a competitor and what will you do when they enter? These basic questions are part of the initial strategic review when thinking about the competition. There may also be some cases where a similar product or service exists that can be substituted for your item. If this is the case, a marketer must review the items that can be substituted as competitive in scope, because a consumer may easily substitute their item for yours.

Understanding and responding to your competition is one way to ensure your market growth. Marketers must be able to assign resources for growth possibilities that often include the reaction to the competition or being pro-active towards the competitive environment. There is always competition in our society and marketers should expect to have competition in the marketplace. Handling the competition must be part of your overall strategy and coming up with ways to deal with competitive issues will help you gain success in the marketplace.

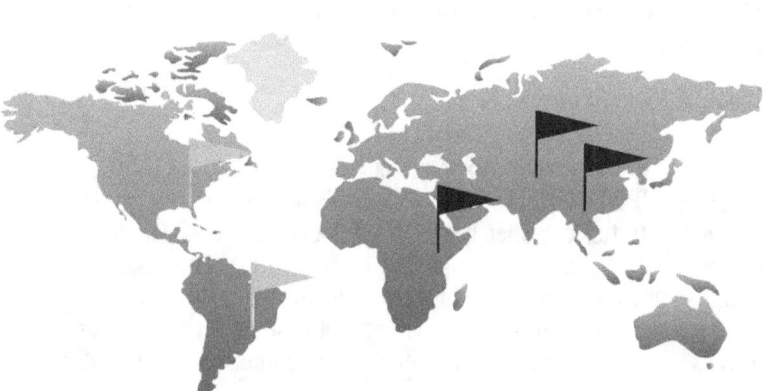

A marketer has to be able to identify the opportunities in the market place. Opportunities are always viewed from an external point of view. In most cases this includes new marketplaces to enter, new geographies, new products to launch, new businesses to buy and entering areas that are not currently being serviced by the market place. Identifying opportunities is vital because proper selection will help to create a road map for your company growth while providing areas to explore when you are ready.

As a marketer looks for the opportunities, they should look where the competition is not, working to fill a market void. Select three to five opportunities in this market void and do the same as if you were the marketer of your competition. Put yourself in your competition's shoes as you review where their opportunities may be based on their Strengths and Weakness. In some cases, you many find that you are both heading in the same direction and in other cases you may see that you're going in completely different directions. In either case, you will want to be prepared to adjust your marketing plan as your business grows based on the strategy.

Lesson #4 : Let's Look at the World.

Marketers have to conduct a review of the macroenvironment of the world to help form their strategy. This review is a test of reality for most marketers. A lack of understanding of how the world is currently evolving around them could mean that a marketer will be left behind.

To review the global macroenvironment, let's look at the **Internet, Social Standards, Legal Issues, Economic Conditions, Political Events and Motivations, and Technological Changes**. You could remember this by using the acronym **ISLEPT.©** A marketer does not want to get caught sleeping so keep a good view on the **ISLEPT©** conditions. As we review these sections of the macroenvironment, we must list any future changes that will positively or negatively affect the marketing strategy.

Internet – The Internet affects every business in the world. A marketer cannot ignore the role that the Internet plays in their business and in the social environment. Social media is now credited for governmental changes ranging from a new president to the take down of a dictator. The Internet is now very powerful and plays a role in daily life worldwide. Marketers must review the Internet and should include e-commerce effects, social media effects and delivery effects on their business and targeted markets. Most individuals and consumers now use the internet to research just about anything, so understanding how these changes online affect your business will help you prepare for them.

Social Standards - Society and culture play a role in our motivations to buy and participate in certain products and markets. A marketer must outline how society and culture play a role in consuming or ignoring a product offering. Roles in society often dictate purchasing patterns and help to define market needs.

Legal Issues – Laws are created to maintain civility and honesty within our marketplace, but sometimes laws are changed to affect the market place. A marketer needs to understand if the product they are offering will be affected by future changes to laws of the market. Creation of new laws are normally a lengthy process. Due Diligence and deep market research normally uncover any possible changes in how a marketer's environment will be changed due to a change in existing laws and addition of new ones.

Economic Conditions – Marketers are often after disposable income. The recession of 2008-2011 eliminated a large portion of personal wealth and affected a large majority of disposable income. Marketers must understand how the economy – good or bad – plays a role in the revenue and consumption of their product or service. Marketers can find opportunity in all market conditions if they plan for them.

Politic Events and Motivations – Often times political motivation translates into new laws that govern business and trade. The political and legal effects are often tied together so a marketer must consider these two environmental factors as a catalyst for a change to their business. The new health law initiated in the U.S. in 2010 was a result of political motivations that changed how companies compensate employees for their health insurance. This created uncertainty in the business world and difficulty in managing a business. Politics can also be viewed in terms of stability within a particular political party. Political instability of parties in power affect most markets and causes volatility in the marketplace for a number of goods and services.

Technological Changes – Technology is identified as " the understanding of the future of your product or service." How will the advancement of technology affect the deliverables of your product? Will technology lower production cost or allow your competitors to be more efficient? These are the types of factors we look for when we review the technology section of the macroenvironment.

Lesson #5 : Know Who your Customers are.

We are always bombarded with marketing messages. Messages like "Try This", "On Sale," "New and Improved," and "Better than the Rest," are always within eye and ear shot. Sometimes these messages are purposely directed at us, while other times they are just randomly displayed. In most cases, you have been targeted as a prospective consumer by a particular marketer. As prospective consumers, we will receive a series of targeted ads based upon our likes and preferences. In the age of the Internet, marketers are now able to narrow these targeted characteristics down to color preference,

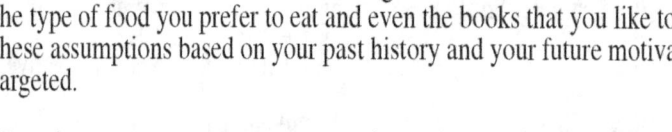

the type of food you prefer to eat and even the books that you like to read. Marketers make these assumptions based on your past history and your future motivations. You have been targeted.

Knowing your customers means getting to know what they like and dislike. A marketer must understand how consumers like to buy their product, when they buy, under what conditions they buy it, where they prefer to buy it and most importantly, why they buy a product. A marketer must know their customer.

Think of your marketing as your only communication tool to your customer. You must say the right thing at the right time in order to get them to do the right thing. How a marketer communicates is important and knowing what to communicate is equally important. This requires research and understanding of your targeted consumer. Research your customers and who they need to be, where they live, how they buy a product similar to yours, why they like any closely related competition and what do your customers want. **Your consumers are your key to success.** Your targeted consumer market will tell you whether or not you have your product right by speaking with their wallets. Your marketing research will identify these targeted consumers and your product sales will speak for itself. If you are successful, your consumers will come back to you and help you to build your business. If you do not understand your consumers, they will not be back for a second try and your business will not succeed.

A target market can be made up of hundreds of thousands and perhaps millions of people. This is known in marketing terms as the "mass" market. The mass market is normally a one size fits all marketplace. In some cases, a marketer can position their product and promote their product under the "one size fits all" mass market with success. To visualize this concept, imagine standing on the roof of a ten story building with hundreds of people standing on the street below. They are all looking up and waiting for you to throw over a sack full of cash. Your cash sack is stuffed with hundred dollar bills. Some of these bills are folded into small squares, some rolled into cigarette shapes wrapped with rubber bands and others are just plain flat hundred dollar bills. The hundred dollar bills in the sack are all the same denomination but each person on the street below prefers to hold their hundred dollar bills a certain way such as in small squares, with rubber bands and straight bills unfolded. When you throw the bills out of the bag off of the roof, the people below collect the bills using their individual preference. Each one of these smaller groups of people would be a "segment" within the mass market. They all collect the hundred dollar bills but each one has a particular preference of how they collect it. They all share similar likes within the large mass of hundred dollar bill collectors.

The smaller "segment" is a group of people that all have similar preferences within the larger mass group. Each unique segment has its own set of likes. Understanding those particular likes will help you to improve your marketing communications to them.

Lesson #6 : Your Price and Position mean something.

Marketers must always accomplish introducing the **right product at the right price**. The challenge marketers face after they have developed the right product is getting to the right price. Consumers will use their wallets to tell a marketer if they have the right price. If your consumers come back to you after the first time, then you have successfully accomplished the right product at the right price. But how do you get to that right price? There are several common ways that most marketers use.

A pricing strategy is important because the right price will help you to generate profits, combat the competition and build your company. The wrong price will result in a failed business plan and strategy. The most common way to price your product is to review your cost and then add your margins on top of this to sell at a profit. This is looked at more closely in the costing section.

Marketers must also consider how the competition is pricing their product. When looking at the competitive price, a new marketer should be to the right or to the left of the competitive price (higher then or lower then). This helps to differentiate the product from the rest of the pack in pricing. Remember that the consumer must believe that the pricing is right and they must believe that they are getting what they expect for that price.

Your product should provide a unique selling proposition (USP) that makes your product different from all of the others. In this case, you will need to adjust your price according to your product positioning. If your product is better performing and higher quality you may want to try to price it higher than your nearest competitor, but if your product is easier, quicker and a better value, then pricing it below your nearest competitor may be the answer. Pricing is an important part of your marketing execution, so take careful consideration with this strategy. Marketers can generally come down in price with special promotions or sales, but rarely have the chance to raise their price. If you make a pricing mistake, make it to the side of the higher price and you can always come down to generate sales.

> # Positioning
> Under Promise.
> Over Deliver.
> Offer Value.
> Offer Quality.

Consumers have a basic understanding of most product prices in many markets. Marketers create this consumer understanding though a strategic and calculated series of marketing communications. The marketing communications help to develop a consumer perception and price reference. Consumers will create a perception of a product when they have been exposed to the communications, purchased a product or been told about a product through word of mouth. The perception of your product in the consumer's mind is defined as "**product positioning.**" The challenge of the marketer is to create a series of communications that help to create this position and give meaning to your price.

Positioning the product requires that marketers meet the basic need of the targeted consumer, create a value for that consumer and deliver on a product promise. Consumers will create a perception in their mind long before they actually spend money on your product. Successful marketers understand that the reality of the product must live up to the perception of the product. Most consumers will regret a purchase decision if they feel that a product did not live up to their promise and meet the preconceived perception that they had in mind. Most of us have heard of the phrase "under promise but over deliver." In the minds of consumers marketers must be careful of the promise they make and over deliver every time.

Lesson #7 : Know your Cost.

The first consideration of pricing your product is to look at your cost. Costs are normally separated into two distinct sections: the **Fixed Cost (FC) and the Variable Cost (VC)**. Fixed Costs include items such as rent, utilities and other expenses that are required to be paid every month regardless of what your business income is. **Variable Costs** are the costs that vary month to month. These costs include how much you pay yourself, any type of one-time expenses, and changes in an item cost needed to operate the business from month to month. **Variable Costs** must be controlled because unexpected expenses in any given month can kill a small company cash flow. Occasionally, marketers include the marketing budget into the variable costs although it probably should be a separate cost line.

Costs also include your **COGS (Costs of Goods Sold)**. These COGS will be the price you pay for the product, the components to make up the product and the service required to handle the product.

Your **Marketing Budget and Expenses (MKTG)** must also be allocated in the expense equation along with **SGA (Selling, General Administration Expenses)**. These expenses can be labor, administrative expenses and miscellaneous business upkeep expenses.

The simple combined total cost equation should look like this:

Fixed Cost + Variable Cost + Marketing Expenses + SGA + COGS = Total Cost

	FC	+	VC	+	MKTG	+	SGA	+	COGS	=	TC
EXAMPLE	$1,000	+	$2,000	+	$2,000	+	$500	+	$400	=	$5,900

Let's Calculate the **Unit Cost** of your inventory:

Once you know your simple **Total Cost (TC)** you will need to divide that into how many units of products you have in inventory to produce a **UNIT COST (UC)**. A Unit Cost will give you visibility into the bottom line price you can get to help you achieve a breakeven point. Assume we have 1,000 units of only one product in inventory using the above TC of $5,900. (Note: Your COGS of each unit is .40 cents ($400/1,000 units=.40 cents)

	Total Unit Cost	**=**	**Total Cost**	**/**	**Number of Units**
EXAMPLE	.59	=	$5,900	/	1,000

Achieving your price is now possible after you know with your Unit Cost are. Add a Unit Profit Margin to your Unit Cost to get to your Final Price. In the example below we added a Unit Profit Margin of 60% to our Unit Cost of .59 cents. This creates the final price of .94 cents.

	Final Price	**=**	**Total UNIT Cost**	**+**	**UNIT Profit Margin (60%)**
EXAMPLE	.94	=	.59	+	.35

(normally a margin of 60% of the unit cost covers most products at wholesale level prices - .59 x 60% = .35)

Lesson #8 : Promote. Discuss. Share.

Consumers are never waiting for a marketer to launch a new business, create a new product or start a new service. If left alone, most consumers will be happy with the current products they have. That is, until the next savvy marketer uncovers a need that is currently going unfilled. **Promotion helps to communicate to the consumer** that a new product has been created. Product promotion is a complete series of targeted communications to a specific group of consumers that need to know about the product. These targeted consumers should be approached with communications such as emails, direct mail, websites, social media marketing, scan bars, samples, TV ads, radio ads, press releases, sales promotions, community events and more. Every point of communication with a targeted consumer should include some type of promotion of the product.

Marketers must explore the best possible way to deliver the promotional message of the product. Factors to consider will be the promotional budget, time of year, target audience, message and call to action. The marketer should always have some type of call to action within their communications. Traditionally, a call to action in a printed ad may be "Bring this ad in for 10% off." In today's communication it may include a direction to a website, a blog or a free download. Promotions are vital to a product because no one will know a product exists unless a marketer tells them. Promotion of the product also varies based on the timing of your product within the product life cycle. Most newly developed products require a significant amount of promotions in the launch of the product while also requiring a regular dose of communication while the product gains acceptance.

Consumers have always researched products that they want to purchase but today they can do it all within seconds from a cell phone. If a marketer is not in this new age of information, then they are out. Consumers will search and decide within minutes by going from Website to Website until they have what they want by price, selection and location. Marketers must maximize every opportunity to capture this business because one dollar lost today can be thousands of dollars lost over time.

The old adage is that "the customer is always right". Marketers know that this is not always the case and most consumers know that occasionally even they get it wrong. Marketing in the new age still requires the basic fundamental principals of customer service, communication and understanding. The challenge for the marketer in **the new age of marketing is communicating with their consumers directly** and in a timely manner. Through the power of the Internet we can instant message, live chat, return call, video call and even trouble shoot problems on line for the consumers. The marketer creates issues when the response rate is slower than reasonable, does not offer an immediate solution or just does not listen to their customer. The new age of marketing requires the human personal touch even through a 15" flat screen monitor or hand held PDA. The key in the new age is to make it honest and timely.

Lesson #9 : Getting Your Product to Market.

We are all consumers. In our lifetime we have purchased everything from schooling to food, from cars to houses, from shoes to hats and from books to music. As a consumer, we have many ways to buy the product we need. Most consumers can buy their products from a retail store, an online store, a buying club or in some cases a distributor. The ways a consumer buys the product is through the channels that the marketer sets up. A marketer must identify how they want to get their product to market for maximum results with as little cost as possible. This is identified as the **Channels of Distribution.**

In today's Internet environment, the channels of distribution for a marketer are often blurred. This results in an opportunity for the marketer to get their product to market a number of different ways. While most large scale marketers choose to be a leader in one market place while using only one type of channel, smaller sized and more flexible marketers may be able to operate a parallel strategy in a number of channels. Different channels require different strategies which also translate into different price points from a retail perspective to a wholesale perspective. Consumers want the best product at the best price but every intermediary that brings that product to market must do so by creating some type of profit for their involvement. A marketer must choose the best channel based on the market demands and pricing demands related to the target consumers and the product.

Marketers generally have four options to get their product to market. The most complicated, most expensive, but often times most profitable, is the direct channel. The direct channel means that the marketer sells the product directly to the consumer. This can be done through an online store, an infomercial on TV or radio, at consumer shows and in some cases in a retail store. The direct approach is the best way to control your marketing message and have hands-on interaction with your consumer. This approach will yield higher profits because you are the maker and the seller but it also requires more investment in time and financial resources.

The second way to bring a product to market would be to sell into retailers. Retailers are valuable because they already have the consumer traffic that will buy your product and they have many resources that can be used to help promote your product. The key to selling to retailers is to remember that putting a product on the retail shelf is one step to success. Getting it off the retailers shelf is the next step to success. Most marketers must have some type of retail support to help them sell the product off of the retail shelf.

The third option would be to sell into a major distributor. These distributors often have close relationships with the retailers and will offer marketing opportunities to promote the product at the retail level. Putting your product with a distributor is like gaining a partner so careful consideration must be made to make sure that the distributor is the partner you will want.

A fourth option would be to work with an agent to help you get into the distributor or the retailer. These agents also have a good network of connections and often times can help by giving you an expert opinion on your product.

Lesson #10 :You Are Your Best Promoter !

A marketer has hundreds of promotional tools available to them. Creating a promotional plan that covers all of the available marketing tools can require large financial resources, hundreds of man hours and lots of creative thinking. Marketers must understand basic fundamental requirements of their product before creating successful promotions. Understanding who wants your product, how they will buy it, when to communicate to them and where to buy it is all part of the process. The communication plan and the promotion of the product is fundamental in the success of the market sell through. Marketers normally have limited financial resources but unlimited marketing visions. **The challenge for most marketers is deciding on what marketing visions are the best** ones and figuring out which ones will bring back the best return on investment.

Marketers should start with a list of ideas. This requires some brainstorming and research. Create a list of the tools that are out there that will make sense to use for marketing the product or service. Not all available tools are reasonable for all products so marketers must be realistic in creating their list of ideas. Putting your product name on the side of a stadium may not be the most realistic opportunity, however sponsoring a local high school team may be. Marketers must evaluate the opportunity to the available resources.

Promoting your business will vary at different levels of the marketing strategy and the size of the market. Marketers should always use Internet tools that are available to them while constructing an "inbound" marketing program. The Internet allows a marketer to promote to prospects 24/7 around the world so promotion on line is vital to a marketer's success. Marketers need to position themselves as problem solvers and experts on line to gain credibility. Consumers will search for your product and they must be convinced that you have the right product that can solve their problem. Promote the products, the management team, and the company through skillfully placed campaigns on line, through community papers, local and regional news channels and popular blogs in your industry

Free is the best price for any product. This is the fundamental difference between public relations and advertising. **Marketers always look for the opportunity to promote their business** through public relations which is generally free to the marketer. Public Relations can come in many forms from press releases to community events but all of these types of marketing opportunities allow for the marketer to be recognized in many ways.

Public Relations is a skill all to itself and does require a full time effort on the part of the marketer to gain proper public exposure. Marketers must understand that a well place public relations story or event can deliver a very high return with little or no investment. Public Relations can be built at all national and regional levels but the local level will help marketers gain traction. Starting a public relations campaign at the local level can include small local charitable donations where you get some mention in a local event article or perhaps the marketer can create some type of special recognition event focused around their product or service. On line public relations will start with creating timely and informative blogs that can be shared with community writers and industry writers. Content is needed in many forms in this fast paced on line world, so good stories about how a product or service improves the quality of life of an individual is a great human interest story.

Do. These 10 Do pages are your hands on lesson. Use these pages to practice what you have learned throughout the book. It may be a bit old fashioned but if you take the time to write down your thoughts about each section that is covered, it will help to formulate your plan. The first step of a plan is to have one. You will need to start by writing down some ideas.

Notes:

The next ten pages include these quick and easy to do exercises:

Action #1 - Create Your Product U.S.P. (Unique Selling Proposition).

Action #2 - Build Your S.W.O.T. (Strengths,Weaknesses,Opportunities,Threats)

Action #3 - Identify Your Opportunity.

Action #4 - Don't Get Caught Sleeping.

Action #5 - Who Are Your Customers?

Action #6 - What is Your Product Position?

Action #7 - What Are Your Costs?

Action #8 - Let's Create Your Promotional Plan.

Action #9 - Are You Ready for Product Launch?

Action #10- Using PR to Promote Your Product!

Action # 1: Create Your Product USP.

A marketer must make their product unique. Consumers expect products to be different in some way and they want this product delivered as promised, on time and within their budget. Marketers must work to let the consumers how their product is different and how their product will meet their demands regularly and without fail. If the marketer does not succeed at this they may have an instant complaint floated on line within minutes of the consumers disappointment. Consumers now have the power to control not only what they buy but also what others will buy as well. Marketers need to carefully craft their marketing position statement so that consumers can immediately get the message. This immediate acceptance turns into revenue. Use the below worksheet to help create your positioning statement.

List three key words or phrases of what your product will do for the consumer:	Identify and describe what type of person your product is made for:
A1.	B1.
A2.	B2.
A3. *Product Benefits*	*Product Target*

Choose three words or phrases that explain your products difference from the competition:	Choose three words or phrases that explain why your product is unique:
C1.	D1.
C2.	D2.
C3. *Product Difference*	D3. *Product Uniqueness*

Choose Two of these marketing strategies:
E1. Low Price   E2. High Price   E3. High Quality   E4. New Tech

Now lets create a USP sentence by using the guide below. Try a combination of the choices above (keeping each letter in it's proper space) to get to one that hits the mark.

_____ will _____ and _____ for
   (Name of Product)   (A1,2 or 3 Product Benefit)   (A1,2 or 3 Product Benefit)

_____ because it is _____ and _____
   (B1,or 2 Target)   (C1,2 or 3 Product Difference)   (C1,2 or 3 Product Difference)

that makes it the most _____ for the _____ and
            (D1,2 or 3 Product Uniqueness)   (E1, 2,3 or 4 Product Position)

_____ consumers.
  (E1, 2,3 or 4 Product Position)

For Free tools, videos and more go to www.30PageUniversity.com   © 2012 ekn links. Ken Ninomiya

Action # 2: Build Your S.W.O.T. .

For each element of the S.W.O.T a marketer must identify a minimum of three points.
A marketer's goal here is to be honest while working toward getting three to five bullet
point items with a brief one sentence explanation of that item for each section.

You should do one of these for each identified competitor (at least three). It is best to complete four separate sheets,
so make three copies of this or download this sheet from www.30PageUniversity.com

Strengths

Weaknesses

Opportunities

Threats

Action # 3: Identify Your Opportunity.

Review the completed S.W.O.T. analysis for your product and the competition. Identify two or three points from each individual analysis and write them into the appropriate box below. When you have completed this step, you will have a review of your product and the competitors. Now do a MOA (Market Opportunity Analysis) using this information. If you see a weakness in your competition that you can compete against successfully circle it. If you see a strength that you have over your competition, circle it. Look for opportunities that you and your competition have. Can you take advantage of any of these opportunities? Circle these. Review the threats to you and your competition. Can you survive all of these threats? Take note of all of the circled opportunities. As you build your strategy, you will need to include these areas.

	Strengths	Weaknesses	Opportunities	Threats
Me				
Competitor #1				
Competitor #2				
Competitor #3				

Write down some of the areas of opportunity circled above. Can you go after these areas?

Action # 4: Don't Get Caught Sleeping.

The world is constantly changing and as a marketer you can not get caught sleeping. Changes within the global environment may effect your business. Below are the factors of ISLEPT. © These are the real everyday factors that affect every global business. List any changes that you can identify, good or bad. Once these possible changes are identified, you will have to understand how they can affect your product. If you recognize an opportunity, you can include this in your strategy for growth. If you identify a possible threat, you can prepare yourself for any possible negative effect on your business. Keep in mind that these global conditions are at a very high level and although they may seem remote to your business today, they may affect your growth tomorrow.

Internet

Social Standards

Legal Issues

Economic Conditions

Political Events and Motivations

Technical Changes

Action # 5: Who are your customers?

People are very different. We all have different needs from one another. Marketers must understand that consumers are people that have unique traits. Among these unique individual traits are also a number of similarities that many of us share. Many of us will have the same type of values, the same type of likes, similar tastes in foods, similar enjoyment in travel, and many other varied aspects of life, culture, family and personal preferences. Marketers refer to these like groupings as "segmentation. Using the chart below, list the traits of your customers within each segment. You can separate each segment by income, geography, age, lifestyle or any other trait you think that will help to define your consumer. After plotting the segments, identify where these customers live (geographic) and how they will buy your product (behavioral).The marketing strategy must be focused on each of your identified segments for maximum success.

	Segment #1 Name of Segment:	Segment #2 Name of Segment:	Segment #3 Name of Segment:
Age, Income, Family Type			
How Will They Buy Product?			
Where Do They live?			
Why would they buy your product?			

Write down your first segment to go after, the message you need to communicate to them to help sell your product, and how you should reach them with your message.

Action # 6: What Is Your Product Position?

Most marketers will find success in selling their product one time to new consumers. The first time consumer is an exciting development in a marketer's world, but the repeat consumer will build the business. Consumers will not come back to buy the product if they believe that there is a disconnect between what the product offers and their perception. How a marketer creates this perception is part of Product Positioning. Positioning plays an important role in helping marketers build a business. The product must meet the needs of the consumer while satisfying the perception of what the product should be. A marketer must position their product in the market place to help the consumer realize this perception.

	High Price Low Quality	High Price High Quality
High Price		
Low Price	Low Price Low Quality	Low Price High Quality
	Low Quality	High Quality

Using this marketing positioning chart, place an "X" on the spot where you think your product will fit into considering price and product quality.

Next, using the three competitors you identified during the S.W.O.T. analysis, place a "A, B, C" on the chart in a spot that best identifies where each of the competitive products will be.

The "X" will represent the position of your product in the market vs. these three competitors.

The ideal place to be on this graph is to the left or to the right of your competitors but never in the middle of them. You want to be different so your quality and price will get you there.

Create a Product Positioning Statement

Using the information on the graph above, write a comparison positioning statement for your product vs. the competition. Example: "Product X is of higher quality but lower priced than product than A, B, or C, which will help to solve all of the consumer's problems."

Action # 7: What are Your Costs?

It will always be difficult to generate a profit if marketers spend more on expenses than their actual sales. A marketer should know how much profit they will make for each unit sold. To calculate this a marketer needs to understand expenses and costs. There are four basic expense categories to manage while planning your strategy. These expenses include the COGS (Cost of Goods Sold) of each product, SGA (Selling and General Administration) expenses, Total Cost (TC), of the operation which includes Fixed Cost (FC) and Variable Cost (VC) and Marketing expenses (MKTG).

The idea is to take the total of all of your cost and divide this into each product to get to a unit costs for each product unit. Marketing plans include a higher level view of financial drivers and should be validated with an accurate financial forecast but this simple equation can be used to make sure that every unit is profitable.

List your Fixed Costs - all cost that occur on a regular basis.	List your monthly Variable Cost.
FC Totals	**VC Totals**

FC Totals + VC Totals = TC

Adding your Total Fixed Cost and your Total Variable Cost will create your Total Cost (TC). This calculation is Fixed Cost (FC) + Variable Cost (VC) = Total Cost (TC).

Selling & General Administration (SGA) will be other selling cost not included in your TC calculation. This cost should not be more then 10% of your unit selling price.

Marketing Expenses (MKTG) is the amount that it would take you to market your product or service. If this is a new product, the allocation for this expense should be 20% of the selling price.

Cost of Goods Sold (COGS) is the cost of each unit of product. This should include all raw cost, component cost, material cost, inbound shipping cost and additional line items that affect the final cost of the product. If you buy a product it will be your total cost of the product into the warehouse.

Take the total of each expense category of TC, SGA, COGS and MKTG and divide this into the current quantity of on-hand inventory of product. Assume you have 100 units of Product X in inventory and your Total Cost is $1,000 then the calculation should be $1,000 (TC) / 100 Units = $10 per unit TC. Apply this similar calculation to TC, SGA and MKTG and place this result in the chart below. Use your actual cost for each individual COGS.

	Example	Your Product
$100	**Unit Selling Price**	
$50	Less COGS	
$10	Less SGA	
$10	Less MKTG	
$10	Less TC	
$20	**Gross Unit Profit**	

Use this chart to calculate your unit PROFIT. Start with your Unit Selling Price of one unit of product. Then deduct all expense lines (COGS, SGA, MKTG, and TC) from one unit of product using the formulas above. The remaining figure is your Gross Unit Profit.

For Free tools, videos and more go to www.30PageUniversity.com

Action # 8: Let's Create Your Promotion Plan.

The Promotion of the product is key to a product's success and is often the only means of communication to your targeted consumer. A strong promotional campaign outlines the plan of communication and what you want to communicate Every promotion should have a goal. There are many ways to spend money on promotional opportunities from postcards to TV advertisements, but there must be a specific reason why we are conducting a communication action. You should never just advertise or promote for the sake of promotion. This is a waste of money. Always have a target audience and a goal in mind. Define who you want to reach, what you want to tell them and why they should buy your product today. Use the chart below to start the promotion outline.

Promotion Tool	Cost Per Month	Date of Promotion	Goal of Promotion
Online Ads			
Social Media			
Local Print			
Local Event			
National Ad			
Radio			
TV			
Online Video			
Other:			

Using your USP and with an understanding of your target consumer, write down your communication message below:

Action # 9: Are you Ready for Product Launch?

Launching a new product before it's time can be a very costly mistake. The market place is a very unforgiving market and consumers will develop a first impression very quickly. Most new products are researched before they are purchased by the consumers on line. The buyers within the marketplace also uses similar techniques while listening to their consumers. A new product must first impress the market maker, who is usually the buyer of the goods and then secondly impress the consumer, who ultimately dictates the success of a new product with their purchases.

Prior to the market introduction, a new product must have a strong strategy and team behind it to help execute the ideas and communication programs required to be successful. Your new product should help consumers solve a problem while fitting into a category that helps them to understand how to buy your product. Complete the questions below to help create your product launch task list.

Who are your target markets and where are they?

Who is the competition and what is their price?

What is your product price and position in the consumers mind vs. competition?

What is your product USP (Unique Selling Proposition)? Why will consumers like your product?

Five steps to a product launch are covered throughout the book and are recapped below:

1. Identify the targeted consumer, competitive items and the market place.
2. Determine market price, product cost, and sales forecast.
3. Create a product USP and explanation of why everyone should buy your product.
4. Develop a strong communication plan.
5. Outline a time line of performance and expectations.

Timeline	Date
Marketing Strategy	
Product Ready for Market	
Promotion Plan Start	
Meet Round One Buyers	
Ship First Orders	

Build a Timeline for Launch with key task as goals. It is always a good idea to keep yourself on a timeline to help manage expenses and expectations.

Action # 10: Using PR To Promote Your Product.

PR is an effective way to promote your company and product at little cost. There is a specific skill to writing effective PR but if you need to create one on your own then you must consider these important guidelines below. In most cases only the first two lines are picked up in online news broadcast so it is important that you say something vital in the first three lines of the release. This PR document can be used for website information, email blast and local interest stories.

Steps to a great PR Piece:

1. Use a powerful actionable headline that draws the reader in.
2. Use a sub-headline to frame the who and the why of the story.
3. Open with your most important "GOTCHA" line within the story.
4. Close with a boiler plate about the company and how more information can be obtained.

> **Headline - under 80 Characters - use strong action words.**
>
> **Sub Headline - under 140 Characters - include company name here.**
>
> **GOTCHA Line - Powerful Statement, name of product, and why consumers need to buy it.**
>
> **Boiler Plate - about your company - 3-4 sentences and website address.**

Identify online PR distribution sites, local magazines, opinion makers, blogs and industry news to send out your PR. Make a list of at least ten targets for the release. Make sure to get the PR to each of this 10 targets and then make a secondary list and then a third to continue to reach more.

Congratulations!

Marketing A Great New Product

CERTIFIED COMPLETION

You have completed the 30 PAGE University Course in **Marketing A Great New Product.**

Your hard work and preparation should help you succeed in the launch of your great new product.

The following additional pages contain worksheets to help you understand the product marketing process even stronger. The Bonus Material section includes lessons, information and a business glossary to help you understand some basic product launch practices and business terms.

Visit us online to register and print out your Completion Certificate for this book.

Every 30 Page University book is supported online with podcast, video lessons, worksheets and additional free tools. Visit www.30PageUniversity.com for more information.

Additional Titles coming soon. Visit us online to sign up for FREE Previews.

BONUS MATERIAL

Please check our website for any material updates www.30PageUniversity.com.

What is Marketing?

There are a series of key questions every marketer must ask themselves to develop a strategy.

Everything is marketed. People, places, things, ideas, products, services and dreams. Marketing started long before the techniques we will discuss in this book were developed. Imagine the Cavemen that had to market fire to one another, explorers had to share and market the benefits of an untapped land, and the founding fathers of America had to help the public understand our new government. Marketing is the foundation of most businesses and can be linked to improvement in the quality of our lives. Marketing is a method of communication to a targeted group of people – the target consumer. Marketing also provides tools to help educate, persuade and offer the targeted consumer a product or service.

Communication is a vital element of marketing and, when used properly, will set the pace for company growth. Communication from marketers can come in many forms, from full color printed messages to text messages under 140 characters. The fundamental idea of communication used in marketing is being able to say the right thing to the right audience. This is considered to be your targeted message to your targeted consumer. A great marketing plan includes a great communication plan.

A marketing strategy should consist of many tools to help create a complete integrated marketing plan. This integrated marketing plan includes communication, deliverables and actions. Your task in developing marketing communications is getting someone else to believe in what you believe in. Your audience will always evaluate the facts and the benefits of your offerings, so your communication should help them to make a choice.

As a marketer your product must deliver a promise to your consumers. This promise will help separate your product from the rest of the pack and should be unique to your product offering. The marketer must deliver on this promise every single time. Consumers expect that the products they choose will meet their daily needs while delivering on their promise of performance. Keep this in mind when constructing your marketing communication plan. Do not over promise.

A marketer needs to work on delivering value, quality and a promise to your consumer that makes your product different. Successful marketing helps to create consumers that choose your product every time. Marketers want to create long lasting loyal relationships with their consumers. Marketers want their consumer to fall in love with them. Building a great marketing communication strategy will help to create this long-term relationship with consumers.

Take a Good Look At Yourself.

Strengths – Internal

Think of a strength as something you do well that not everyone else can do. This strength is a core part of your marketing plan and can be considered a core competency. A core competency is something that you do better than anyone else, something that would be difficult to copy and something that you can build your business on. A marketer should be able to come up with three to five internal strengths.

This same thought process must be applied to the top three competitors in the marketplace. A marketer must list the strengths of their identified competition. It's a good idea to be able to identify three to five traits that your competition does well that may give you trouble in the future. Identifying these areas will help you understand how to defend against your competition.

Weaknesses – Internal

A weakness, simply stated, is the opposite of a strength – something you do not do well at all. This is often hard to identify from the entrepreneurial point of view because most entrepreneurs think they do everything great. In fact, if you are reading this book maybe your marketing savvy is a weakness. A marketer must look at the internal weakness such as experience, knowledge, resources, and other items that are a weakness. Once you have identified three to five weaknesses for this section, you should also do the same for at least three of your competitors. When you examine your competitor's weaknesses you want to identify areas where you can focus your strengths to capitalize on their potential weakness.

Threats – External

A marketer must know that competition is always a threat. Marketers also know that the macroenvironment plays a role in how their business is affected. A marketer must look past the competition as a threat. External elements like changes in culture, economies, needs and supply will threaten any business. If you have a core competency then the threat of not being able to complete that core competency can close your business. Every marketer has threats that will severely affect their business model. Identifying these threats will be key to helping you prevent them, mitigate them and plan for them. A marketer must also take a look at how their competition views their threats by listing them just as you would for the competitive strengths.

Measure Your Customers and Your Risk.

Best Case Scenario
Sell 150 Units
Make Profit
Grow Business

Acceptable Scenario
Sell 100 Units
Break Even
Keep Business

Worst Case Scenario
Sell 50 Units
Lose Money
Business Unknown

You have a great product and now you want to market it. But how many people will think it's great and buy it? Quantifying your target is essential to understanding the execution of the strategy. If you think that 100 people will buy your product then you need to estimate how much revenue and profit you will obtain from these 100 customers. This is "forecasting" your estimated revenue. A marketer needs to know this because it will help to validate the business strategy and also help to allocate the necessary resources needed to get to execution.

It is the marketers job to evaluate the possible market scenarios and to use these scenarios to help with a forecast. Using a three level scenario is often the best way to lay out your forecast strategy. To do this a marketer should estimate a worst, acceptable and best case scenario. To illustrate this point lets use the 100 units sold as the acceptable scenario. If you sell 100 units, you will generate enough revenue to pay for the cost of the products, the expenses of the business (including marketing) and leave room for profit to put in your pocket. The worst case scenario would be 50 units, which will put you in the red and force you to take money out of your pocket to keep the business going. The best case scenario would be selling 150 units, which will provide for all of your expenses, generate profits and also leave money for business growth.

If you cannot quantify the market with acceptable numbers to cover your business overheads and provide for a profit, you must re-evaluate the business. Marketers must decide on the market to enter and forecast out the quantity of units sold that will allow for the business to break-even and generate a profit. If a marketer cannot satisfy the bottom line number needed to be profitable, then a change must be made in the product, the market or the position of the product. Remember, great products can sell themselves once but great marketing can sell great products over and over again, eventually building a business and possibly a brand.

Growing the Business.

WHAT DRIVES SALES?

Sales are increased through an integrated marketing communications plan that is part of the marketing strategy.

To build a business and to build brands, marketers must keep consumers buying their product. Marketers must decide how to build sales. To do this they rely on the market conditions but these conditions need to be primed for growth. Marketers must quantify the who and the where of the targeted consumer so that they can forecast sales and expenses.

Growing your market is the foundation to growing your business. Marketers must anticipate the growth of the market. If you cannot grow your market, then you will have a one time shot to make a profit.

There are several ways a marketer can grow the business. The first most obvious way is to keep getting new customers. To get new customers, you must always promote your product. Making new customers aware that your product exist allows a marketer to have a solution for the consumers current need. Gaining new customers means penetrating your existing market or entering new markets. Every customer gained will add to the bottom line.

A second way to grow your business will be to create a new product that compliments and enhances the offering of your first product. This means that you must also create a marketing strategy for that product and hope to be able to maximize your current customers into the new product. In this case, a marketer will win both ways.

Buying a competitive line is another way to grow your market. This strategy requires a completely different set of objectives and is often the most costly way to gain market share but grows your business and eliminates the competition in one shot.

The last way to grow your business is by selling more products to your existing customers. This is where the marketer must really do their homework. A marketer can increase sales with promotions, service, and updated versions. Changing the marketing mix will often help the marketer achieve better results to their existing customer base.

In all cases of growth, a marketer must be able to anticipate and plan for growth. Marketers should not be on the short end of the stick when the great product they have turns into a full fledge running business. A fully operational business requires resources and planning. Not understanding your growth will quickly put the brakes on it.

30 PAGE UNIVERSITY

It's All in the Packaging.

In marketing we use the four P's (Product, Place, Promotion and Price) to guide us. The "Product" also covers **packaging** but this "P" should be a topic of it's own. Packaging is often over looked as a last minute thought but could be one of the main reasons why products fail. Consumers do judge a book by its cover and products are also judge by their packaging. Poor packaging can kill a product.

If you are selling a product into a retail, wholesale or consumer environment is important to have great packaging because consumers must feel that they are getting value when they make a purchase. The packaging for a $200 item should make the consumer feel like they just spent $200. The packaging of a product allows consumers to educate themselves about the product before they make a purchase. Consumer will often compare products based on what they see from the outer packaging. This means that your product packaging has to convey the correct message to the consumer every time.

Your labels on your packaging should always conform to legal standards, but keep design of the package and label in mind. It does not have to be ugly. Labels are informational and help the consumer want your product - use action words to convey the message.

Packaging is unique for most products. Examine the competitive items or like items before you design your package. Keep in mind that if you want to replace a competitive item you have to create a similar pcakage with the same type of size and design to fit onto the retail shelf. Always get opinion makers involved before deciding on your final design and get the help of professionals to design the package.

Packaging a product for retail includes offering the consumer a visual of why the product is made just for them. The packaging should convey the fact that your product will help solve a specific consumer issue. Illustrating that the product will make life easier while providing a solution should also be demonstrated on the package.

Take time to construct a smart package when designing the product packaging. Include simple "BUY ME NOW" type of language on the front of the package, more complicated explanation of "WHY THIS PRODUCT IS FOR YOU" on the back of the package, and additional cross-selling or promotional information on the sides of your package. A box package can have as many as four billboards to promote your product so make sure you use them wisely.

The Internet is A Business Tool.

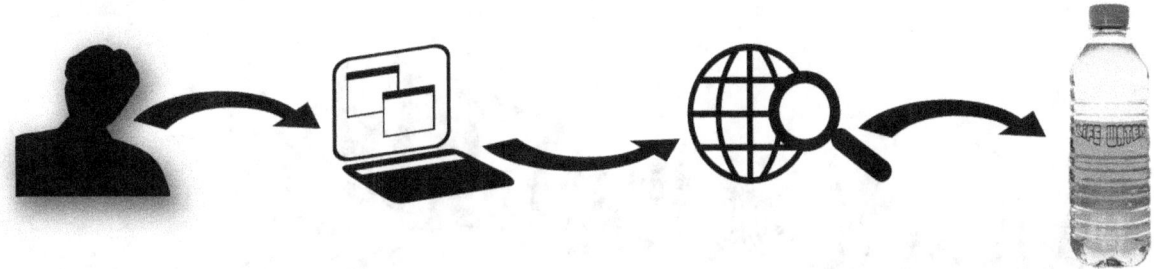

The Internet hardly is twenty years old, yet it has changed the way most of us live our daily lives. Marketing has gone from one way communication to a newly developed two way communication transferring more power to the consumer over the marketing messaging every day. All marketers must embrace the Internet from day one and this includes web sites, social marketing, key word marketing, blogging, video casting and texting. In fifteen years, marketers are still understanding all of these new communication tools. They also are working to understand their power while taking their consumers along for the ride.

Consumers expect a marketer to be on line. There is no reason why any business, product or service today should be without a web site, a blog, and a series of social network accounts. Costs for all of these necessary marketing tools on line have come down to under $10.00 per month to manage and in some cases there is no cost to participate with online marketing tools. The most basic Internet items to have will be a dynamic web site, a blog, a social networking account and a video account. All four of these Internet tools are as easy to use as any basic computer program and can be set up by any single individual or by a trained contractor.

A marketer's web site must be engaging, fun to be on, easy to read and informative. Most visitors to any web site like to get to the information one click from the home page. Keep this in mind when designing your web site. Keep the information easy to read and easy to get to. Web sites that sell products online require careful planning and a professional should be consulted when designing the site so that you can help your consumer get to what they want quickly.

Another Internet tool to have will be a basic blog. Blogs are useful tools to help the marketer spread the word about the product and the company. Marketers must also be connected to one of the many social networking web sites available by creating business and fan pages. Social marketing is the word of mouth marketing that is required to help build a buzz about the product. Lastly, the marketer should create a video or photo channel on line. Videos are being watched by consumers and a great video can be your best online spokesperson 24/7.

Every new product launch requires a specific product strategy that also fits into the overall company strategy. If the new product is out of place from the current product portfolio, it is a good idea to review the strategy to validate that it can make sense moving forward. Most companies should have a strong marketing plan that outlines the overall company strategy and most new products should be aligned within this overall plan. A well constructed marketing plan can be the heart of the business so marketers must take time out to put one together.

Use the following marketing plan outline to help with the write-up of the marketing plan. The marketing plan is the direction of most businesses and a new product should have a very specific plan that will help it to be successful within it's defined target market.

The Marketing Plan

Marketing Plans come in many different formats but there are standard requirements for all plans. Listed below are Nine Important elements that all marketing plans require.

I.   **Executive Summary** - The Executive Summary appears at the beginning of the plan, but is always written last. This section should summarize your plan with enough information in only two or three pages of detail.

II. **Situation Analysis** - What problem are you solving? What need are you filling?

   Include in this section:
   a. Market Summary - Define the market. Why is this market attractive and how big is it?
   b. S.W.O.T. Analysis - What is the analysis of your product and company?
   c. Competition - Who are the competitors? What is each of their S.W.O.T.?
   d. Product - Identify each product specifically. What is your USP?
   e. Keys to Success - What are the most important factors to making your plan successful?
   f. Critical Issues - What must happen to make sure you are a success?

III. **Strategy**

   a. Marketing Objectives - Meeting these marketing objectives should lead to sales.
   b. Financial Objectives - Outlines your financial future with a 3 year outlook.

IV. **Target Market** - Who is the target? What are the Needs/Benefits sought by the market?

V.   **Pricing** - Review product price and costs for accuracy and market positioning.

VI. **Distribution** - Identify the most effective methods for getting products to market.

VII. **Promotion Mix** - Describe the potential promotional programs and the media choices.

VIII.**Sales Forecasting** - Project sales and income for next three years.

IX. **Action Plan** - Prioritize all strategies by levels of importance.

   a. Controls help you measure results and identify any problems or performance.
   b. Contingency Planning - How will you handle difficulties, problems and risks?

Worksheet #1 - Building A Brand.

Use this checklist to help you build your product into a brand. Answering these questions is a great place to start in understanding what your brand and product is all about. Knowing where your brand is vs. the competition is vital to communicating your uniqueness to your consumers.

Answer the following questions:

1. How does your largest competitor position their brand against yours?

2. What is your competitor's marketing message? How is it different from yours?

3. What marketing promise does your competitor make?

4. Do your competitors deliver on their marketing promises?

5. What are the benefits of using your product or service vs. the competitor?

6. What promises does your company make during the marketing process and do you deliver on those promises?

8. Does your customer or your clients believe you are delivering on your promises?

9. What can you do today to deliver a better benefit and promise to your customers? Can you take customers away from your competition with this promise?

Work Sheets

Worksheet #2 - The Launch Sheet.

Launching a product is very difficult and requires careful planning. As part of the marketing strategy it is important to understand the launch basics. This simple list represent the marketing mix for a new product launch. Careful planning will increase the level of success for any new product launch.

Provide simple answers to each point. Go Back to the drawing board if you can not complete with a simple one line statement. This means you have not narrowed the product down to make it simple.

PRODUCT

1. Product Name

2. USP

3. Customer Target Profile

PACKAGING

4. Packaging Function

5. Packaging Label and Design Features

6. Packaging Message - Call To Action

PLACE

7. Channel Selection

8. Sales Strategy for Channel

9. Support needed for Channel

PRICE

10. Competitive Pricing Comparison

11. Costing Analysis - Do you know cost?

12. Final Price and Profit Review

Worksheet #3 - Product Packaging

Product packaging is the silent salesman. The packaging of your product will help the consumer understand the product. If you are hoping to sell your product at a high price, then the packaging must transmit that high quality value. Most marketers who launch a product for the first time do little to make their packaging look good. The extra effort and additional time a marketer puts into their packaging before the product is launched will result in a higher level of success.

The list below is an outline of key factors a marketer must consider when creating a new package for a new product.

1. **The Product Name.**
   Make sure that another company does not have that name already.
   Make sure that the name makes sense to the consumer.
   Make sure that the product name fits the category.

2. **The Right Colors and Design for Your Package.**
   Colors help to sell on the store shelf. Test them to make sure it is pleasing to your consumers.
   Keep it clean and simple - don't over design and put large amounts of information on package.

3. **Package Label Design and Regulatory Information Requirements.**
   Most products require UPC and product identifiers and some may require federal regulatory mandates. Make sure your design is simple but conforms to all laws and requirements.

4. **The Right Size Package or Quantity of the Product.**
   You may need to adjust your current package to provide different sizes for the right channel.

5. **Socially Conscience and Environmentally Friendly Qualities of your Package.**
   You will need to work on keeping your package minimal in components to meet some standards.

Worksheet #4 - Product Check List

The process of creating a new product for the market is very complicated. There are numerous steps to take along the path of success. Every idea should be tested before the idea is put into production. This means that a prototype should be developed, used and tested before going into final production. The first place all new products should start at is with a legal patent check to make sure that the idea is not already out there. Most ideas need to be protected and after reviewing the patents in the market a new idea should get it's own. Patents are just the start of the new product check list. The list below offers a checklist of steps that all product launches should go through before hitting the market.

Event	Comments-Results
☑ 1. Product Name	
☑ 2. Product Descriptions	
☑ 3. Product Customer Target	
☑ 4. Unique Selling Proposition	
☑ 5. Product Patent Check	
☑ 6. Prototype One Creation	
☑ 7. Test of Prototype One	
☑ 8. Review of Prototype One Testing	
☑ 9. Second Prototype after first review with revisions	
☑ 10. Testing of Prototype Two- Review - Final Feedback - Final Product Prototype	
☑ 11. Production and Timeline Review	
☑ 12. Product to Production Round One and Test of production	
☑ 13. Round One Production and Review	
☑ 14. Consumer Testing Final Production	
☑ 15. Go or No Go Into Manufacturing and Launch	

Glossary for Marketing A Great New Product

Action Plan - The action plan lists and prioritizes all the marketing strategies and activities identified.

Advertising (Promotion) - The placement and purchase of persuasive messages in any mass media.

Aging (Inventory on Store Shelf) - The length of time merchandise has been in stock at a retail store.

Affordable Budgeting - The amount spent on Promotions after all other necessary expenditures are paid for.

Audience - The persons who are exposed to a particular type of advertising media (Target Market).

Behavior Segmentation - Focuses on occasions, user status and useage rates of your target market.

Barcode - An application that uniquely identifies various aspects of product characteristics. (UPC Barcode)

BOGO - A "Buy One Get One" Free promotion used to spur quick sales from a retailer.

Brand - A name, term, design, symbol, or unique feature that identifies a good or service distinct from others.

Brokers - An independent sales agent who helps to sell your product to their account base within a territory.

Budget - The detailed financial breakdown of a strategic plan that allocates resources and manages expenses.

Buying Calender - A specific time frame that a buyer will buy a product line or review new product.

Cash Terms - Includes a discount for a payment within a period of time.

Certificate Of Insurance (COI) - Insurance policy maintained by the manufacturer on behalf of the retailer to cover those manufacturer's products sold by the retailer directly to the consumer.

Channel Of Distribution (Place) - Intermediaries that help to perform all functions required to move product.

Circulation - the number of copies of a print advertisement that are distributed.

Community Relations - Interactions with the local communities.

Competition - Rivalry among sellers of the same or similar products.

Glossary for Marketing A Great New Product

Co-op Funds - Product promotional resources used to support retailer advertising programs paid to channel.

Consumer - The end user of goods or services.

Consumer Behavior - The behavior of the consumer in the market place towards a product.

Consumer Characteristics - The demographic characteristics of the consumer. (Age, Income, Race, Etc.)

Consumer Satisfaction - Meeting or not meeting consumer's expectations.

Contingency Planning - "Plan B" or developing alternative plans to the main plan.

Convenience Product - A product (such as toothpaste, bread, and milk) that is bought frequently on impulse, with little time effort spent on the buying process.

Copyright - A copyright offers protection to the owner of original work that is printed.

Culture - The set of learned values, norms, and behaviors that are shared by a society.

Customer - The actual or prospective purchaser of products or services. (also Buyer or consumer)

Database - Information on current and prospective consumers and customers.

Demand - The number of units of a product sold in a market over a period of time.

Demographics - Characteristics of consumers- Age, Income, Education, Sex or Occupation

Direct Marketing - Directed toward a specific targeted group – products sold without any intermediaries.

Direct Manufacturer Sales Team — The company hires their own sales team and leadership including account executives to manage all trade customers.

Display - A special exhibit of a product, in addition to any standard shelf representation.

Distribution - (Place)- The marketing and carrying of products to customers.

Glossary for Marketing A Great New Product

Distribution Fee - A fee charged by wholesalers / chains for initial retail product placement.

Exit Strategy - Refers to a plan that the manufacturer would have in place to handle discontinued items from current inventory with a retailer.

Extended Terms - Additional dating terms in support of distribution of product.

Feature - The use of advertising, or other activity, to call special attention to a product.

Focus Group - A method of gathering beliefs of consumers through group interaction that usually focuses on a specific topic or product.

Forecasting - In forecasting sales, or other objectives, a variety of statistical models are used and available, offering insights otherwise difficult to obtain. Estimate numbers of units to be sold over a specified period of time.

Guaranteed Sale - A contractual agreement between the retailer and manufacturer that insures unsold product can be returned to the manufacturer.

(GTIN) Global Trade Item Number – This is an assigned number to the specific product of each manufacturer. This number must be purchased through an authorized agency.

Key Success Factors - Necessary conditions for success in a given market.

Life Style - The manner in which people conduct their lives.

Local Market Broker Representation - Hired sales specialists within a specified market that will help sell product to retailers.

Macroenvironment - The global external conditions facing a company.

Market - The actual amount of product users and customers.

Market Area - A geographical area containing the customers and users.

Market Demand - The total volume of a product bought and used by a specific groups in a specified market

Market Development - Expanding into a new market with a set of existing products or services.

Market Penetration - Expanding sales to your current market. Occasionally accomplished through a promotional campaign, which include pricing the same product or service below the competition. To gain additional sales.

Glossary for Marketing A Great New Product

Market Positioning - Consumer perceptions of the product, the price, value and quality.

Market Research - A series of activities designed to identify customer needs and wants, and recording and analyzing of data with respect to a particular market.

Market Segmentation - Subdividing a market into distinct subsets of users that behave in the same way or have similar needs.

Market Share - The total sales in a market obtained by a product.

Market Skimming - This strategy involves setting the price for your product or service high in order to "skim" the market demand with a long term strategy of lowering prices to meet market demand.

Marketing - The process of planning and executing the conception, pricing, promotion, and distribution of ideas, goods, and services to create exchanges that satisfy individual and organizational goals.

Marketing Mix - The mix of controllable variables used to reach the target market, including price, product, place and promotion (the 4 P's).

Marketing Opportunity - An attractive market area that a product is likely to have a competitive advantage.

Markup - A percentage based on the cost of the product multiplied by one plus the percent of markup desired.

Me Too Pricing (Follower Pricing) - Using a "follow-the leader" approach and setting prices in response to all major competitors.

Mission Statement - An expression of a company's managerial goals that tells the world what business they are in.

MSRP (Manufacturer Suggested Retail Price) – This is the price that is suggested to sell for at the retail level. At times it is the actual price and at other times it is the Value Price.

Non-production Cost - Costs include overhead expenses, marketing expenses, and the profit margin required by the business to cover total costs.

On-line vendor Portals - Websites that contain information about how to do business with that retailer or allow business transactions with that retailer.

Pay-On-Scan - The process of payment to the manufacturer by the retailer when products are scanned (sold) at store level.

Glossary for Marketing A Great New Product

Penetrated Market - Actual set of current users within a product market.

Penetration Pricing - Artificially lowering your price to gain market entry over your competition.

Perception - The impression that is formed of "reality" and guides personal choices.

Point of Difference - This explains how your product is different and why the product will sell.

Point-of-Purchase - (POP but sometimes POS) Promotional materials placed at retail to attract product sales.

Point-of-Sale (POS) - A data collection system that electronically receives information from a sales transaction.

Pricing - Calculating cost, expenses, and profits while comparing to market conditions and competition.

Price Protection - Manufacture agrees to reimburse the retailer for any drop in price (cost) of the product.

Pricing Strategies - Various price strategies used to complement business goals. The most common are penetration, skimming, and follower pricing.

Primary Research - Original and direct research that you get first hand.

Product Audit - Conducting an in-depth question-and answer session about product performance and customer wants and needs.

Product Claims - What your product will do and where you stand relative to the competition.

Product Life Cycle - The four stages products go through : introductory, growth, maturity, and decline.

Product Mix - The full set of products offered by an organization.

Product Positioning - The way consumers view brands of products. A perception of value and quality.

Production Costs (COGS)- Costs include labor costs and material costs. Cost Of Goods Sold (COGS).

Profit - The amount left after production costs and non-production costs are subtracted from gross revenue.

Promotional Calendar - This is a timeline of the product promotions and marketing plan - normally 12- 18 months out.

Glossary for Marketing A Great New Product

Promotion Mix - The various communication techniques such as advertising, personal selling, sales promotion, and public relations/ product publicity.

Psychological Factors - Includes personality types (introverted or extroverted), attitudes (degree of enthusiasm for a particular product) and the importance of a particular purchase.

Public Relations – Non-paid form of communication to influence feelings, opinions or beliefs about the product.

Retailer Due Diligence – A manufacturer's research to gain retailer's understanding of customer specific needs and their category requirements.

Quality Control - An ongoing analysis to verify if products meet specified standards.

Questionnaire - A document that is used to ask questions about products.

Reference Group - A group that the individuals use evaluating his/her own beliefs.

Retailer Form – An informational form that all product manufacturers must fill out to get their product placed into a retailers system and sold within channel.

Secondary Research - Using already published surveys, books, magazines, etc. to analyze the information in them in terms of your proposed product.

Self Service - The customer is exposed to merchandise (browsing without assistance)

Shopping Good - More time is spent selecting this product because it is shopped for..

Situation Analysis (S.W.O.T.) - An examination of the internal factors that identify strengths and weaknesses, and the external environment to identify opportunities and threats.

Slogan - The verbal or written portion of an advertising message that summarizes the main idea in a few memorable words--a tag line.

Slotting Fees - The consideration given to the retailer by the manufacturer for placement of item with the retailer.

Glossary for Marketing A Great New Product

Social Factors - Social factors can focus on life-style (homebody, workaholic), social class or brand loyalty, among others.

Social Advertising - Advertising designed to motivate target audiences to undertake socially desirable actions.

Specialty Advertising - The placement of advertising messages on things like calendars, coffee cups, pens, hats, note paper, T-shirts, etc.

Specialty Good - Consumers will spend more time searching for this type of special product.

S.R.P. - Suggested Retail Price - This is the Suggested Retail Price offered to the final consumer.

Stakeholder - All users, employees, board members, vendors or other who have a relationship with the product.

Strategic Market Planning - Decisions on how a business can compete in the markets that is usually based upon the totality of the marketing process.

Stock Keeping Unit (SKU) - Refers to the actual product being sold by the manufacturer to the retailer.

Target Market - A particular segment of a total population that is focused on.

Total Cost - Includes expenses, manufacturing, distribution, capital, labor and overhead. This normally includes fixed cost (FC) + variable cost (VC).

UPC Number - (Barcode) This is a specified number assigned to the product and to the manufacturer that will identify the product when scanned through a retailer system. This number must be purchased by an authorized agency.

Vision - A guiding theme that expresses the nature of the business and product.

Vendor Information – This is required information about the manufacturer, the sales, the product and additional information required to be part of a retailers system.

Word of Mouth Communication (WOM) - Occurs when people share information about products or promotions with friends- greatly used in social media today.